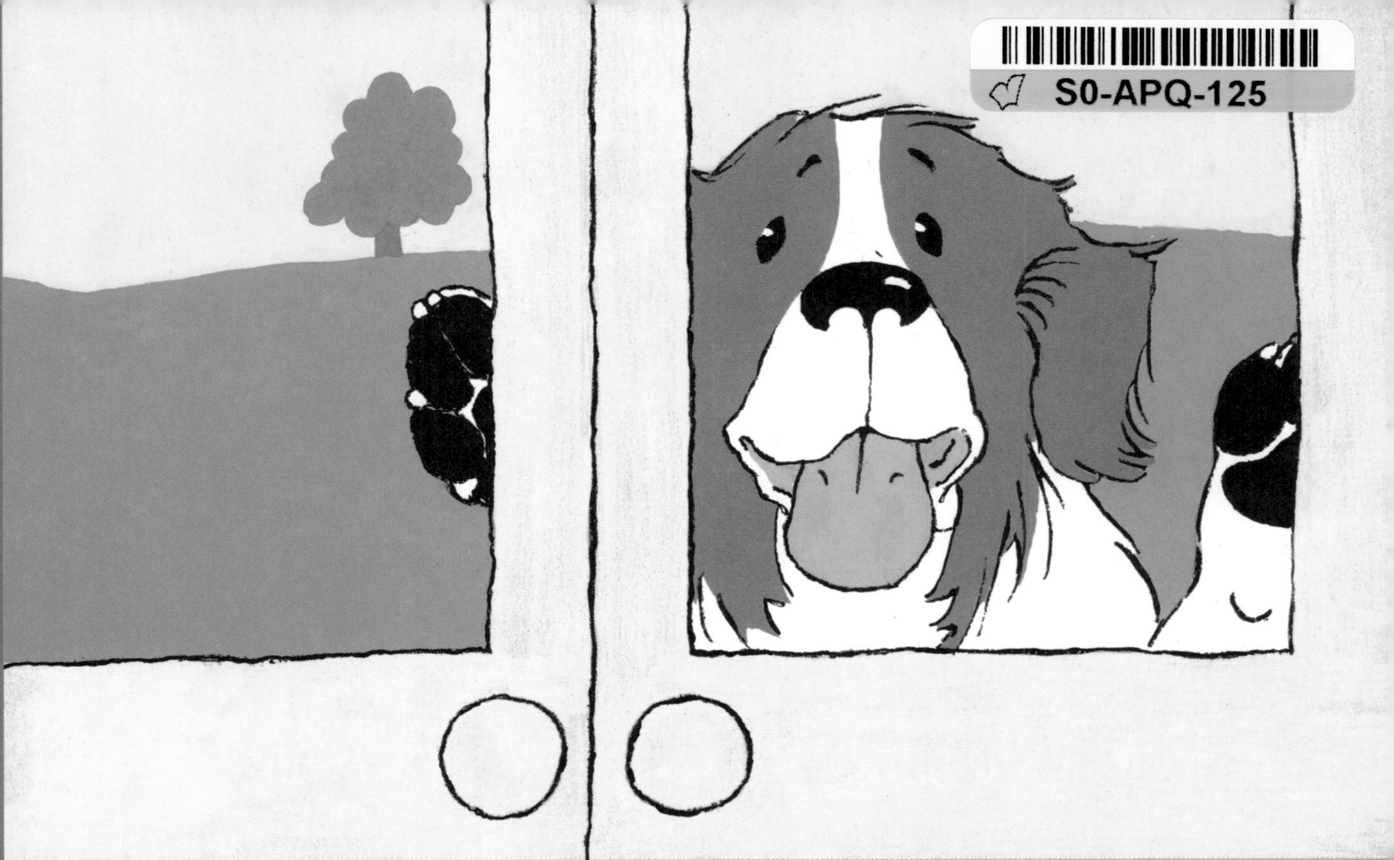

Winnie wants to come in.

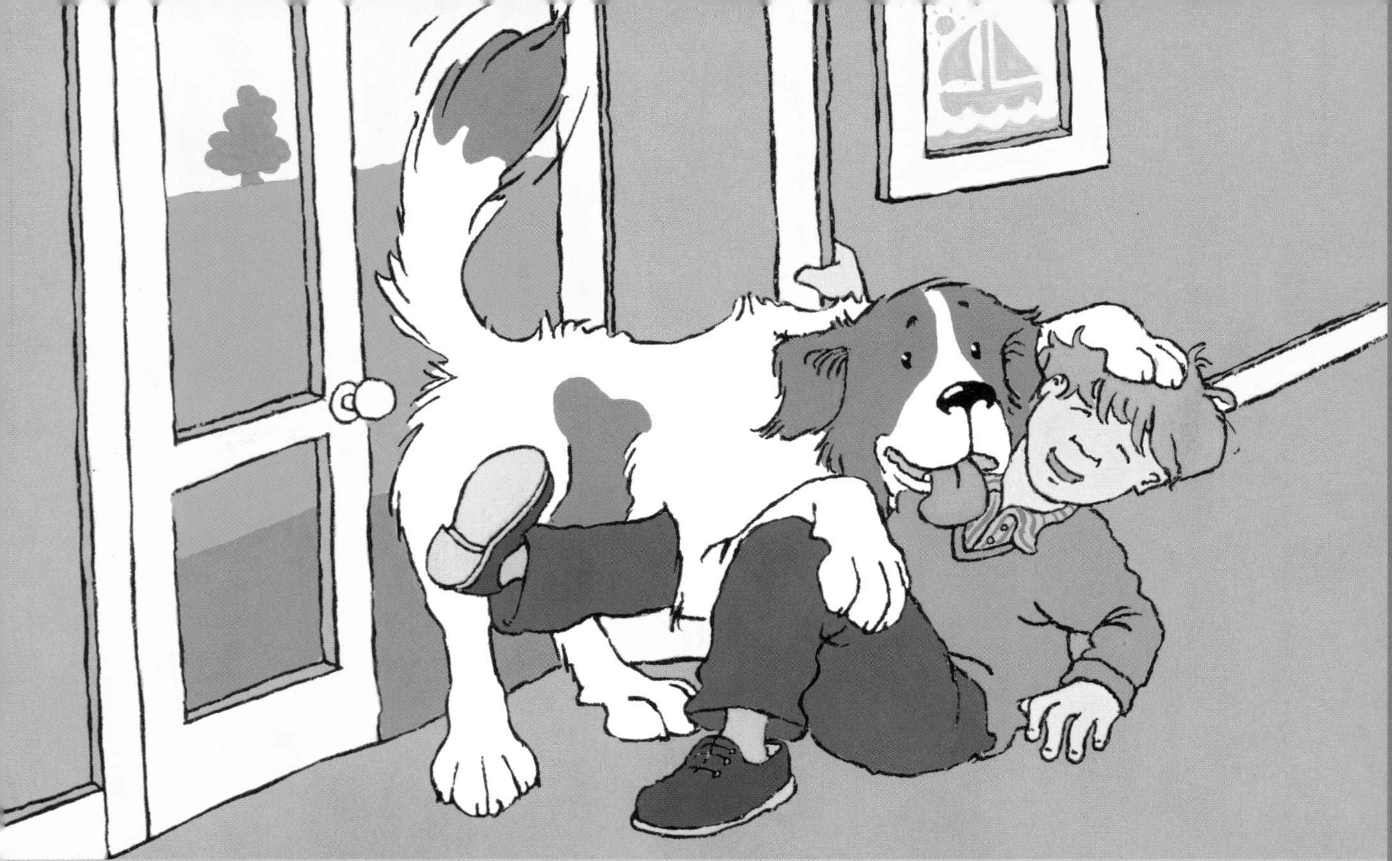

Daddy lets her in.

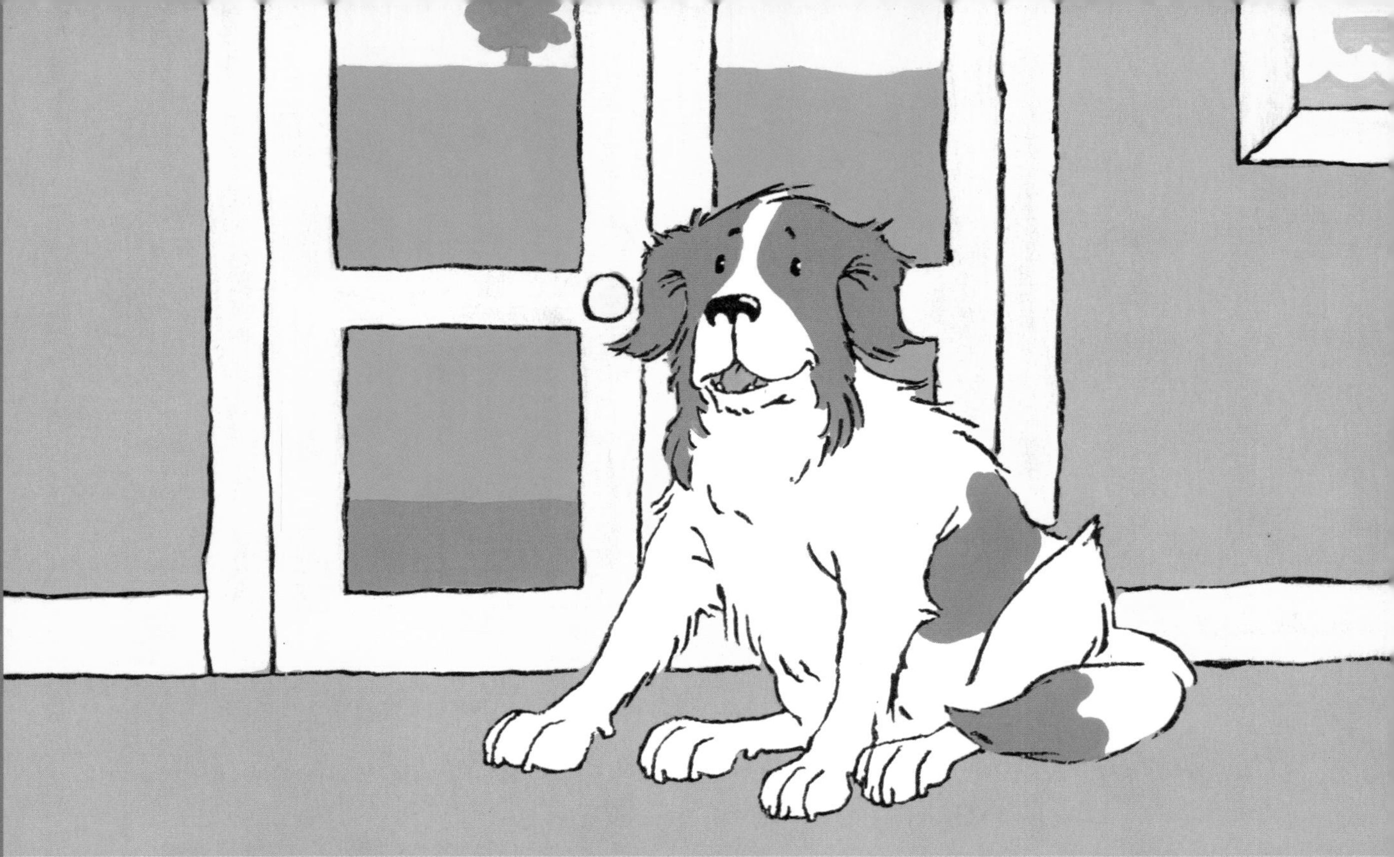

Winnie wants to go out.

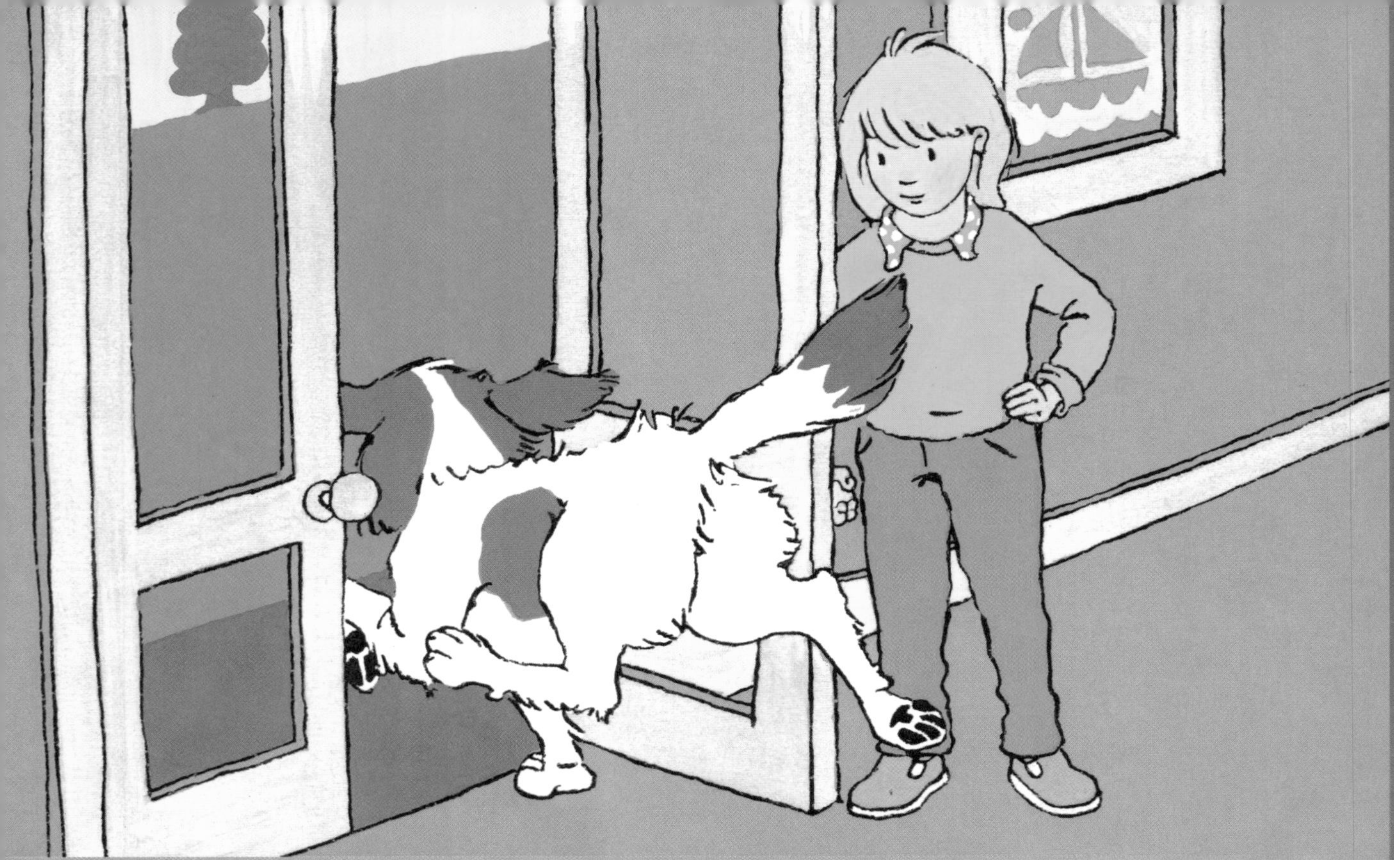

Mommy lets her out.

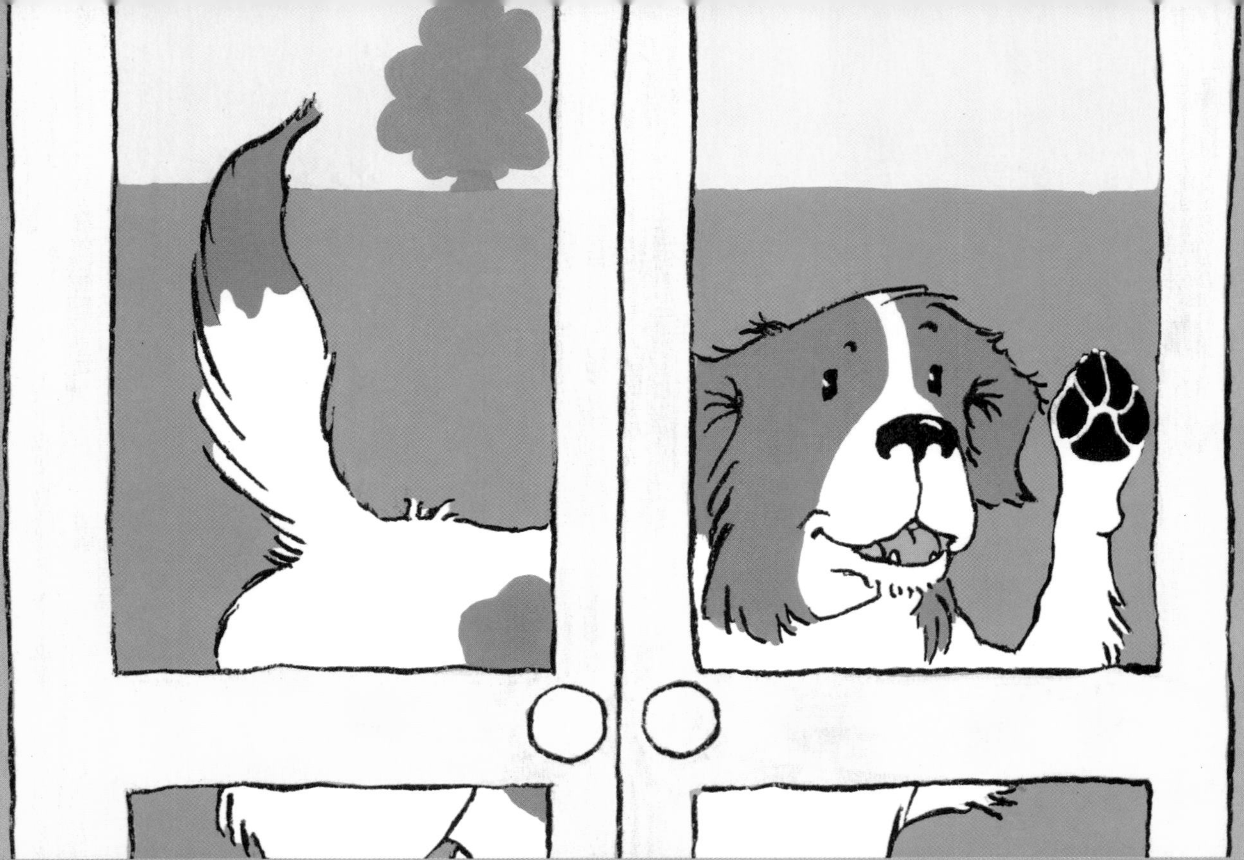

Winnie wants to come in.

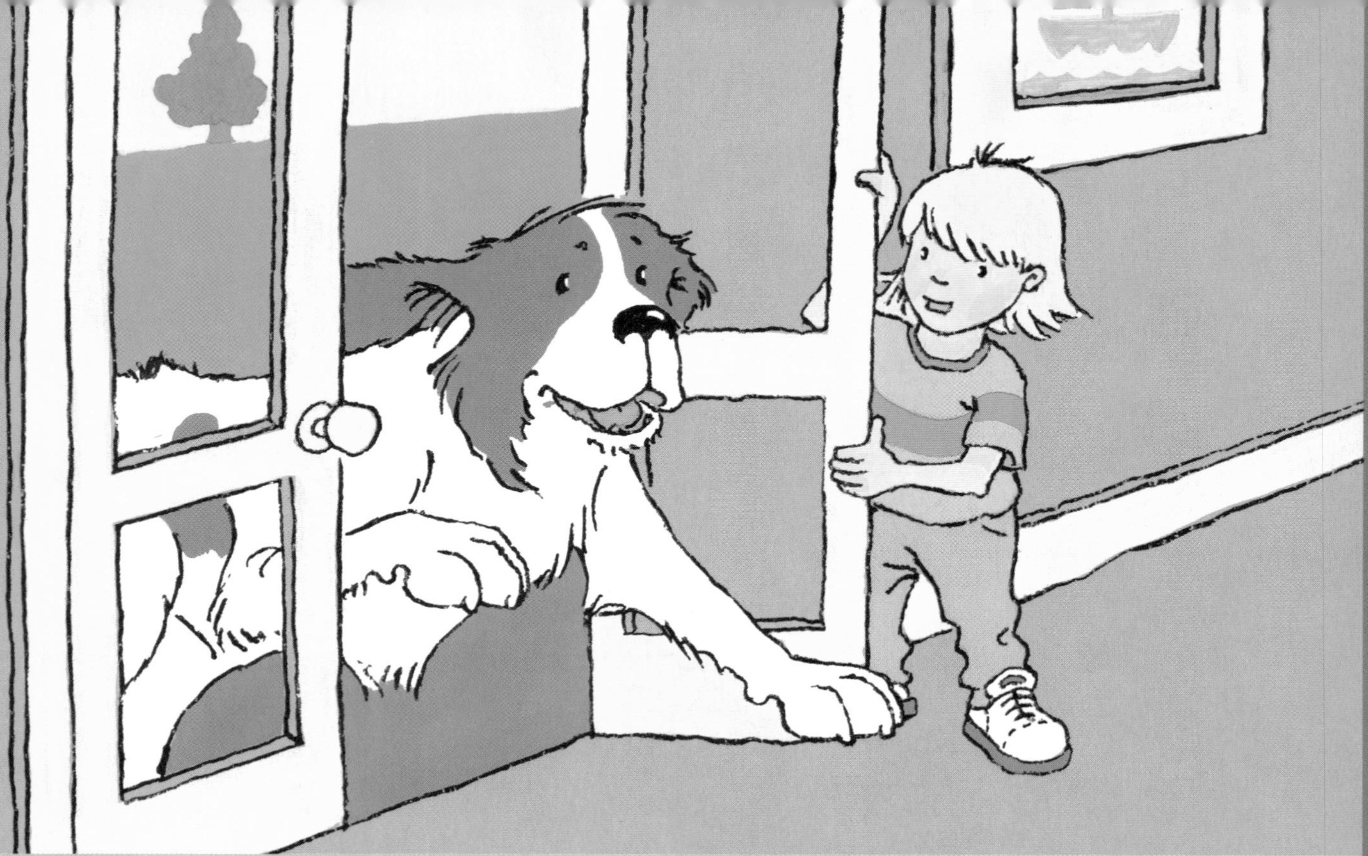

Annie lets her in.

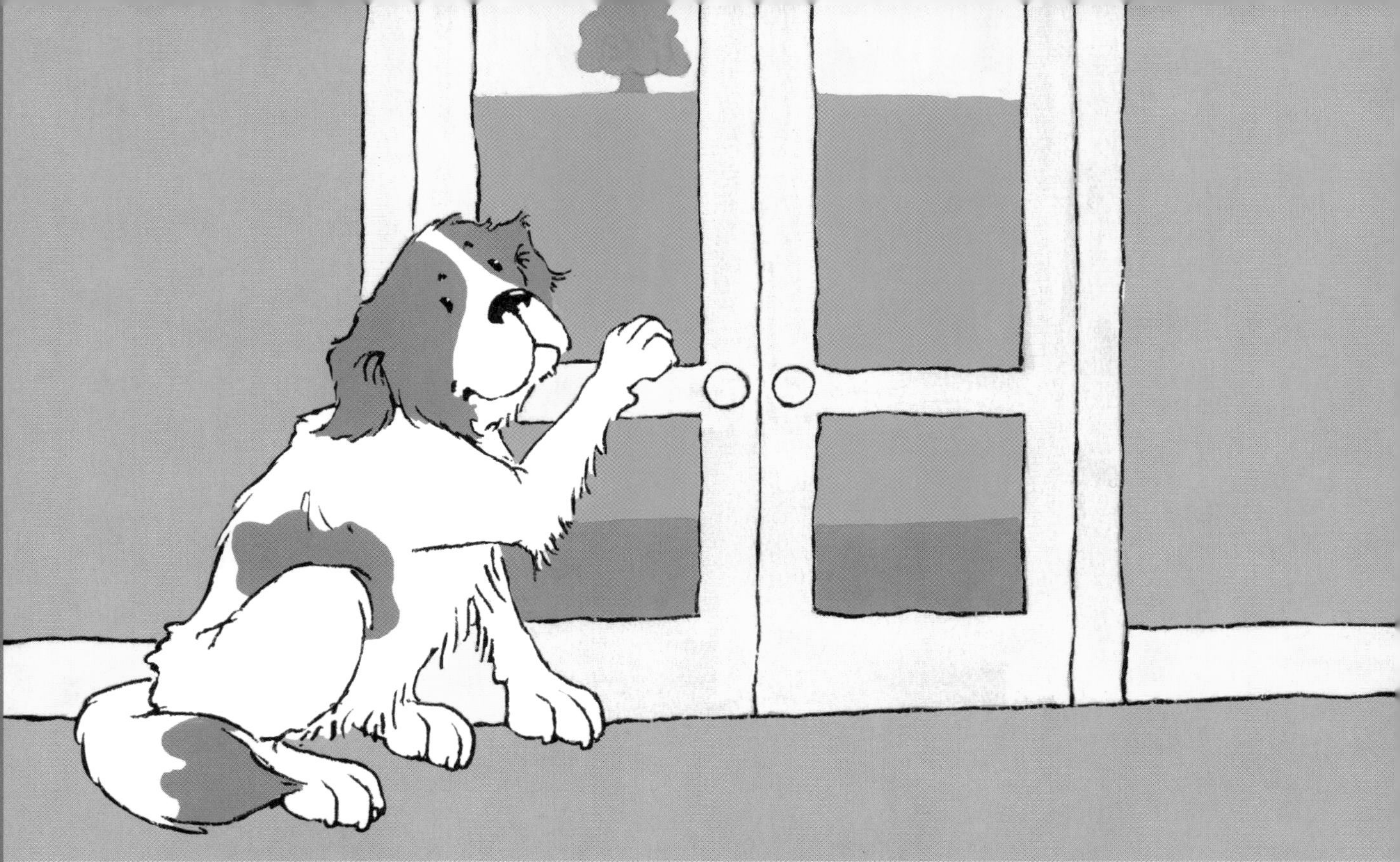

Winnie wants to go out.

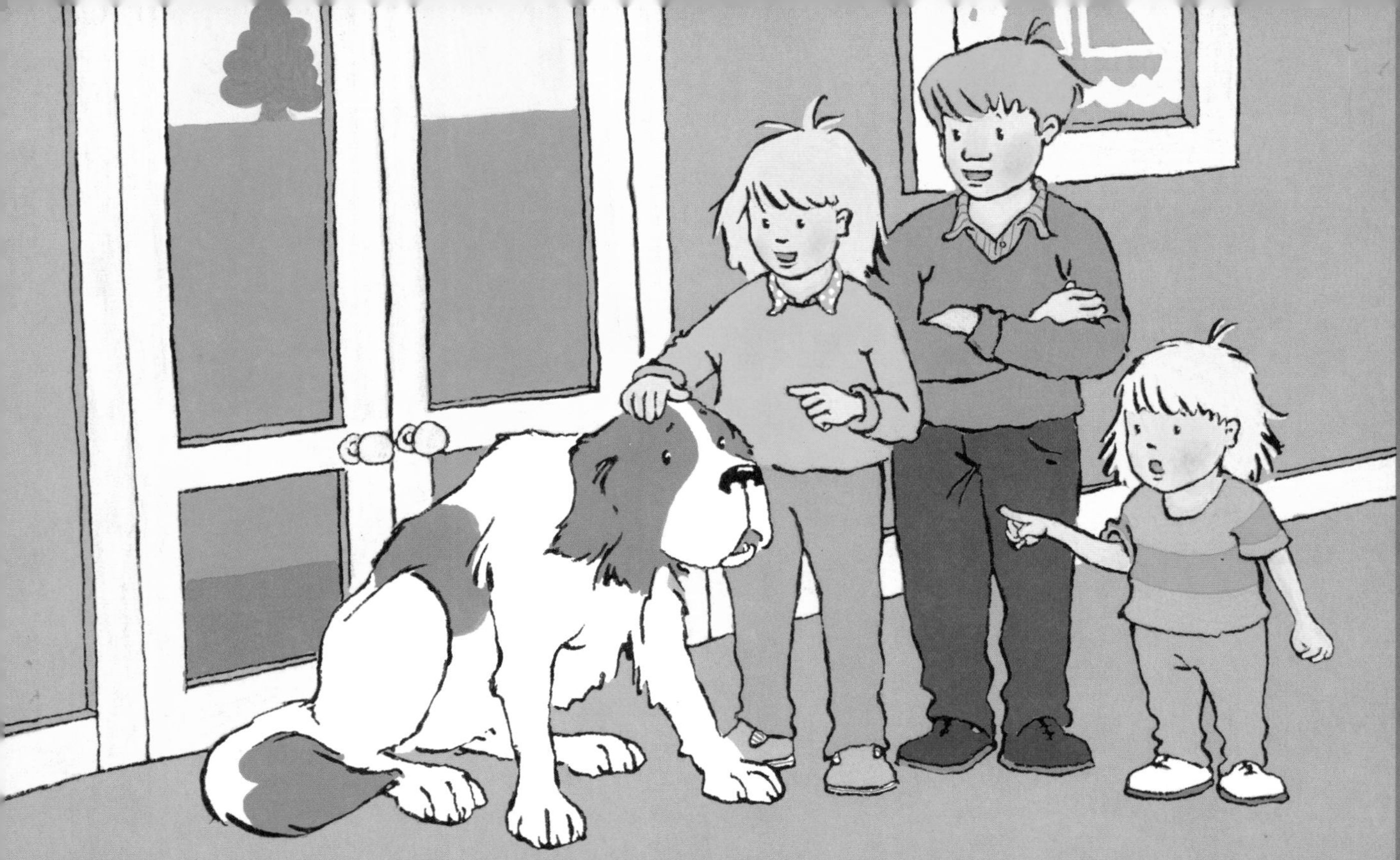

"NO!" say Mommy, Daddy, and Annie.